D1488036

SHERLOCK
HOLMES
CHILDREN'S COLLECTION

SHADOWS, SECRETS AND STOLEN TREASURE

AR

POINTS_____

BOOK LEVEL_____

TEST #_____

Published by Sweet Cherry Publishing Limited
Unit 36, Vulcan House,
Vulcan Road,
Leicester, LE5 3EF
United Kingdom

First published in the US in 2019
2019 edition

2 4 6 8 10 9 7 5 3 1

ISBN: 978-1-78226-581-8

Sherlock Holmes: The Naval Treaty

Cover design by Arianna Bellucci and Rhiannon Izard
Illustrations by Arianna Bellucci and Sarah Hoyle

www.sweetcherrypublishing.com

Printed and bound in India
I.TP002

SHERLOCK HOLMES

THE NAVAL TREATY

SIR ARTHUR CONAN DOYLE

Sweet Cherry
PUBLISHING

In July of 1883, Sherlock Holmes took on one of his biggest cases yet. By this time, Holmes was so famous that he was often engaged in cases of international importance. Some of these involved senior figures from Britain's royal and political families, so I am forbidden from making the details public. But this case was unique. The security of the nation was at serious risk until Holmes unraveled a problem that had baffled both the police and the government. The treaty it concerns is now public, so there is no harm in telling this tale.

During my school days, I had a friend called Percy Phelps. He was a brilliant boy. Although he was about the same age as me, he was two classes ahead. I remember that he won several prizes at school and then a scholarship to Cambridge University. His mother's brother was Lord Holdhurst, a great Conservative politician, but this famous relative did him no good at school. I'm very ashamed to say that I took part in some of the teasing he received on the playground.

Since then, I had forgotten him entirely until the following letter arrived:

Briarbrae, Woking

My dear Watson,

I am sure you remember 'Tadpole' Phelps who was in the fifth form when you were in the third. You may have heard that, through my uncle's influence, I got a good position working in the Foreign Office, and that I was well respected until a horrible disaster occurred.

There is no use writing of that dreadful event. If you agree to my request, it is better that I tell you myself.

The stress of it made me very ill for nine weeks, and I am still very weak. Could you bring your friend Mr. Sherlock Holmes down to see me? The authorities assure me nothing more can be done, but I hope desperately that he can help. Do try to bring him down, and as soon as possible. Every minute seems like an hour when I live in this horrible state of suspense. Assure him that I did not ask for his advice earlier because I have been unable to think clearly until now. Now I am a little better, although I dare not think of it for fear of a relapse. I am still so weak that I have to have someone else write this for me. Do try to bring him.

Percy Phelps

There was something pitiable in the repeated pleas to bring Holmes. I was so moved that I would have done anything to help him myself. I knew that Holmes loved his art and was always ready to help clients who truly needed him. Within an hour of finishing my breakfast, I was back once more in our old rooms on Baker Street.

Holmes was seated at his table, wearing his dressing gown and working hard over a chemical experiment. A rounded glass vessel was boiling furiously in the bluish flame of a Bunsen burner. Drops of liquid were condensing into a jug. My friend hardly glanced up as I entered. Seeing that his investigation must be important, I sat down in an armchair and waited.

Holmes dipped into this bottle and that, drawing out a few drops of each liquid with his glass pipette, and finally brought a test tube containing a solution over to the table. In his hand he held a slip of litmus paper.

"You come at a crisis, Watson," he said. "If this paper remains blue, all is well. If it turns red, it means a man's life is in danger."

He dipped it into the test tube, and it flushed a dull, dirty red.

"Ha! I thought as much," he cried. "I will be at your service in an instant, Watson." He turned to his desk and scribbled off several telegrams. Going to the door, he called downstairs for a waiting lad and gave them to him. Then he threw himself down into the chair opposite me and drew up his knees until his fingers clasped around his long, thin shins.

"A very commonplace little murder," he said. "You've got something better, I fancy. What is it?"

I handed him the letter,

which he read with the utmost concentration.

"It does not tell us very much, does it?" he remarked as he handed it back to me.

"Hardly anything."

"And yet the writing is of interest."

"The writing is not his own."

"Precisely. It's a woman's," he said, nodding. "And a woman of rare character. You see, at the beginning of an investigation it's good to know that your client is in contact with someone extraordinary, whether good or evil. My interest is already awakened. If you are ready, we will go to Woking and see this politician with a problem, and the lady to whom he dictates his letter."

We were lucky enough to catch an early train at Waterloo, and in a little under an hour, we found ourselves among the fir woods and heather of Woking. Briarbrae was a large detached house standing on extensive grounds near the station.

We were shown into an

elegantly decorated drawing room where we were joined in a few minutes by a rather stout man. His age may have been nearer forty than thirty, but his cheeks were so red and his eyes so merry that he looked like a mischievous schoolboy. He vigorously shook our hands with a big smile. I was

surprised at his rather over-
friendly manner, considering the
reason for our visit.

"I am so glad that you have
come," he said. "Percy has been
asking for you all morning. Ah,
poor old chap. He is desperate. He
clings to any straw."

"We have had no details yet,"
said Holmes. "I see that you are
not a member of the family."

The man looked surprised, and
then, glancing down, he began to
laugh.

"Of course, you saw the J. H.

16

monogram on my tie," he said. "For a moment I thought you had done something clever. My name is Joseph Harrison. Percy will soon marry my sister, Annie, so we shall be relations by marriage. You will find my sister in his room, for she has nursed him for two months. Perhaps we'd better go in at once, for I know how impatient he is."

The room into which we were shown was on the same floor as the drawing room. It was furnished as a combined bedroom and sitting room, with flowers arranged daintily in every corner. A young-looking man was lying upon a sofa by the open window, through which came the rich scent of the garden and the balmy summer air. He looked pale and worn.

A woman was sitting beside him and rose as we entered. "Shall I leave, Percy?"

He clutched her hand to stop her from going.

"How are you, Watson?" he said. "This, I presume, is Mr. Sherlock Holmes?"

I introduced him with a few

words, and we both sat down. The
stout young man had left us, but
his sister still remained with her
hand in that of the invalid. She
was a striking-looking woman,
with a beautiful olive complexion,
large, dark, Italian
eyes, and thick
black hair.

Her Mediterranean appearance made the white face of her companion seem more worn and haggard by contrast.

"I won't waste your time," he said, raising himself on the sofa. "I was a happy and successful man, Mr. Holmes, when a sudden and dreadful misfortune wrecked all my prospects.

"I was, as Watson may have told you, employed at the Foreign Office. When my uncle, Lord Holdhurst, became foreign minister, he trusted me with several important missions. I always carried them out successfully, so he came to have complete confidence in my ability and tact.

"Nearly ten weeks ago, on the 23rd of May, he called me into his room. He praised me for all the work I had done recently and then gave me a new task."

Phelps broke off his narrative and reached into a cabinet next to the sofa, placing the book he had been reading inside. I glanced at Holmes, who hadn't moved since Percy had begun. His eyes were dreamy, and I knew that he was already processing the information we had heard so far, which was really only the background to the mystery.

"Lord Holdhurst then went over to his bureau and took a roll of gray paper out of a drawer. He spoke to me earnestly.

"'This is the original secret treaty between England and Italy. Unfortunately some rumors of it have

22

already got into the press. It is
of enormous importance that
nothing further should leak
out. The French or the Russian
embassies would pay a large sum
of money to learn the contents
of these papers. Normally they
would not leave my bureau, but
it is absolutely necessary to have
them copied. Take the treaty and
lock it up in your desk. I shall
give directions for you to remain
behind when the others go. That
will allow you to copy it at your
leisure without being overlooked.

When you have finished, lock both the original and the copy in the desk, and hand them over to me personally tomorrow morning.'"

Percy looked at us earnestly. "I took the paper and–"

"Excuse me an instant," said Holmes. "Were you alone during this conversation?"

"Yes."

"In a large room?"

"Thirty feet each way."

"In the center?"

"Yes."

"And speaking quietly?"

"My uncle's voice is always very quiet. I hardly spoke at all."

"Thank you," said Holmes, shutting his eyes. "Please go on."

"I did as he said and waited until all the other clerks had gone. One of them in my office, Charles Gorot, had some work to finish, so I left him there and went for some dinner. When I returned, he was gone. I was anxious to get on with my work because I knew that Joseph was in town and that he would travel down to Woking by the eleven o'clock train. I wanted to catch it if possible.

"When I looked at the treaty I saw that my uncle had not exaggerated its importance. It was related to the Triple Alliance. As you gentlemen know, each country in this alliance promised to support each other if there was an attack by any other great power. The topics in this treaty were to do with the navy. At the end were the signatures of very high-ranking people.

"I then settled myself to the

task of copying it. It was a long document, written in French. It was twenty-six sections long. I copied as quickly as I could, but at nine o'clock had only done nine sections. It seemed hopeless to attempt to catch my train. I was feeling drowsy, partly from my dinner and partly because of the long day's work. I thought a cup of coffee would clear my brain. A commissionaire has a little alcove at the foot of the stairs and is in the habit of making coffee at his stove for any of the officials who are working late. I rang the bell to summon him.

"To my surprise, it was a woman who answered the bell. She was a large, coarse-faced, elderly woman. She explained that she was the commissionaire's wife, so I asked her to make me some coffee.

Commissionaire
Trustworthy and true, these are usually retired or injured members of the armed forces who find employment as doormen or security officers. They are very loyal to their employers. Astute and observant, they make ideal witnesses.

"I wrote two more sections, and then I rose and walked up and down to stretch my legs. My coffee had not yet come and I wondered what the delay could be. Opening the door, I started down the dimly lit corridor. This corridor is the only exit and ends in a staircase with the commissionaire's alcove at the bottom. Halfway down this staircase is a small landing with another passage running into it at right angles. This second one leads to a side door, used by clerks as a shortcut when coming from Charles Street. Here is a map of the place."

He handed us a piece of paper with a neat drawing showing the parts of the building he had described.

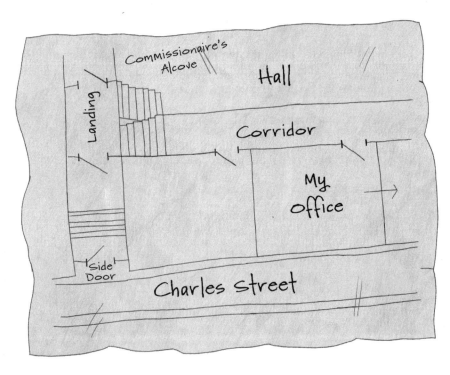

"Thank you. I think I follow you," said Holmes.

"This is where the mystery begins," went on Phelps. "I went down the stairs and into the hall. There I found the commissionaire fast asleep in his alcove with the kettle boiling furiously on the stove. I took the kettle and turned off the stove, for the water was spurting onto the floor. I was about to shake the sleeping man when a bell over his head rang loudly, and he woke with a start.

"'Mr. Phelps, sir,' he said,
looking at me in bewilderment.

"'I came down to see if my coffee
was ready,' I said.

"'I was boiling the kettle when
I fell asleep, sir.' He looked at me
and then up at the quivering bell
with a stare of astonishment.

"'If you was
here, sir, then who
rang the bell?' he
asked.

"'The bell!' I cried. 'What bell is it?'

"'It's the bell of the room you were working in.'

"A cold hand seemed to close around my heart. Someone was in that room where the precious treaty lay upon the table. I ran frantically up the stairs and along the passage. There was no one in the corridor, Mr. Holmes. There was no one in the room. Everything was exactly as I left it except that the treaty had been taken. The copy was there and the original, gone!"

Holmes sat up in his chair and rubbed his hands together. I could see that the problem had caught his interest. "What did you do then?" he murmured.

"I realized that the thief must have come up the stairs from the side door. I would have met him if he had come the other way."

"You were sure that he could not have been hidden in the room, or in the corridor?"

"It is absolutely impossible. A rat could not hide himself either in the room or in the corridor. There is no cover at all."

"Thank you. Please go on."

"The commissionaire, seeing my pale face, had followed me upstairs. Now we both rushed along the corridor and down the steps that led to Charles Street. The door at the bottom was closed but unlocked. We flung it open and rushed out.

I clearly remember that as we did so there came three chimes from a nearby clock. It was a quarter to ten."

"That is of enormous importance," said Holmes, making a note on his shirt cuff.

Miss Harrison offered Phelps some water. He paused to take a sip.

"The night was very dark and a thin, warm rain was falling. There was no one on Charles Street but a lot of traffic, as usual, on Whitehall. We rushed along the pavement and at the far corner we found a policeman.

"'A robbery has been committed,' I gasped. 'A document of great value has been stolen from the Foreign Office. Has anyone passed this way?'

"'I have been standing here for a quarter of an hour, sir,' he said. 'Only one

person has passed during that time – a tall, elderly woman with a Paisley shawl.'

"'Ah, that is only my wife,' cried the commissionaire, 'has no one else passed?'

"'No one.'

"'Then the thief must have gone the other way,' cried the fellow, tugging at my sleeve.

"But I was not satisfied. The attempts that the commissionaire made to pull me away increased my suspicions.

"'Which way did she go?' I asked.

"'I don't know, sir. I noticed her pass, but I had no special reason for watching her. She seemed to be in a hurry.'

"'How long ago was it?'

"'Oh, not very many minutes.'

"'Within the last five?'

"'Well, it could not be more than five.'

"'You're only wasting your time, sir,' cried the commissionaire. 'Take my word that my old woman has nothing to do with it, and come down to the other end of the street. Well, if you won't, I will.'

And with that, he rushed off in the other direction.

"But I was after him in an instant and caught him by the sleeve. 'Where do you live?' I asked.

"'Number 16, Ivy Lane, Brixton,' he answered. 'But don't be led astray by a false scent, Mr. Phelps. Come to the other end of the street and see if we can hear anything.'

"Nothing was to be lost by following his advice. With the

policeman, we hurried down, only to find the street full of people coming and going. All were eager to get to their destinations on such a wet night. There was nobody lingering whom we could ask.

"Then we returned to the office and searched the stairs and the passage without result. The corridor that led to the room had cream linoleum that shows marks very easily. We examined it carefully but found no footprints."

"Had it been raining all evening?"

"Since about seven."

"How is it then that the woman who came into the room about nine left no traces with her muddy boots?"

"I'm glad you raised that point. It occurred to me at the time. The cleaning ladies are in the habit of taking off their boots at the commissionaire's alcove and putting on soft shoes."

"There were no marks then, although the night was a wet one? The chain of events is certainly one of extraordinary interest. What did you do next?"

"We also examined the room.

There is no possibility of a secret door, and the windows are thirty feet from the ground. Both of them were fastened on the inside. The carpet prevents any possibility of a trapdoor, and the ceiling is of the ordinary whitewashed kind. I would bet my life that whoever stole my papers came in through the door."

"How about the fireplace?" asked Holmes.

"There is none. There's a stove. The bellpull hangs from the wire just to the right of my

desk. Whoever rang it must have come right up to the desk to do it. But why should any criminal wish to ring the bell? It is a most bizzare mystery."

I waited for Holmes to contradict him. No mystery is unsolvable to my friend.

"Certainly the incident was unusual," Holmes said. "What were your next steps? You examined the room, I presume, to see if the intruder had left any traces – any cigar butt, dropped glove, hairpin, or other trifle?"

"There was nothing of the sort."

"No smell?"

"Well, I never thought of that."

"Ah, the scent of tobacco would have been worth a great deal to us in such an investigation."

"I never smoke, so I think I would have noticed any smell of tobacco. There was no clue of any kind. The only real fact was that the commissionaire's wife – Mrs. Tangey – had hurried out of the place. Her husband could give no explanation except that it was about the time when she always went home. The policeman and I agreed that our best plan would be to seize her before she could get rid of the papers – if she had them.

"The alarm had reached Scotland Yard by this time. Mr. Forbes, the detective, came round at once and took up the case. We hired a hansom cab. Within half an hour we were at the commissionaire's house. A young woman, who proved to be Mrs. Tangey's eldest daughter, opened the door. Her mother had not come back yet, so we were shown into the front room to wait.

"About ten minutes later there was a knock at the door. Here we made a serious mistake. Instead of opening the door ourselves, we allowed the girl to do so. We heard her say, 'Mother, there are two men in the house waiting to see you.' In an instant afterwards we heard the patter of feet rushing down the passage.

"Forbes flung open the door and we both ran into the kitchen, but the woman had got there before us. She stared at us with defiant eyes, but then suddenly recognized me. An expression of absolute astonishment came over her face.

"'Why, if it isn't Mr. Phelps, from the office!' she cried.

"'Who did you think we were when you ran away from us?' asked Mr. Forbes, the detective.

"'I thought you were the debt collectors,' she said. 'We have had some trouble with a tradesman.'

"'That's not a good enough answer,' answered Forbes. 'We have reason to believe that you have taken an important paper from the Foreign Office and that you ran in here to dispose of it. You must come back with us to Scotland Yard to be searched.'

"She complained, but we did not

listen to her. A cab was brought, and all three of us drove back in it. We had first made an examination of the kitchen. We were careful to check the kitchen fire, to see whether she might have thrown the papers when she was alone. There were no signs, however, of any ashes or scraps.

"When we reached Scotland Yard, she was handed over to the team to be searched. I waited in an agony of suspense until they came back with their report. There were no signs of the papers."

At this point in the story, Phelps looked so desolate that my heart went out to him. Holmes' face showed a mixture of excited anticipation with just a hint of pity. No doubt he expected to solve the mystery and clear Phelps of the crime.

"For the first time, Mr. Holmes," he continued, "the horror of my situation came in its full force. Until then I had been so sure of getting the treaty back at once that I had not dared to think of what would happen if I failed. Now there was nothing more to be done except think of my position. It was horrible. I thought of my uncle and his colleagues in the Cabinet, of the shame that I had brought upon him and everyone connected with me. Even if this were an extraordinary accident, no allowances are made for accidents when diplomatic interests are at stake. I was ruined – shamefully, hopelessly ruined.

"I don't know what I did, but I must have made a scene. I have a dim memory of a group of officials

crowding
round, trying
to help me.
One of them
drove me to
Waterloo and
got me onto the
Woking train.
Fortunately
Doctor Ferrier,
who lives near

me, was on the same train, and
he took charge of me. It was good
that he did, because I had a panic
attack at the station and was

almost raving mad by the time we reached home.

"You can imagine how things were when they were awoken by the doctor's ringing and found me in that condition. Poor Annie here was broken-hearted. Doctor Ferrier had heard enough from the detective at the station to be able to give them an idea of what had happened. It was obvious to all that I was not going to recover quickly, so Joseph was bundled out of this bedroom. Then it was turned into a sickroom for me.

"I have lain here for over nine weeks, suffering from brain fever. If it had not been for Miss Harrison and for the doctor's care, I should not be speaking to you now. She has nursed me by day and a hired nurse has looked after me by night. Slowly my reason has cleared, but it is only during the last three days that my memory has returned. Sometimes I wish that it never had.

"The first thing that I did was to write to the detective, Mr. Forbes. He assured me that everything had been done, but no trace of a clue had been discovered. The commissionaire and his wife were examined without any light being thrown upon the matter. The police also suspected Gorot, the clerk who, as you may remember, stayed late in the office that night. But I did not begin work until he had gone. Mr. Forbes found nothing to implicate him in any way.

"I turn to you, Mr. Holmes, as absolutely my last hope. If you fail me then my honor as well as my position are forever lost."

He sank back upon his cushions, tired out by this long speech. His nurse poured him out some medicine.

Holmes sat silently with his head thrown back and his eyes closed. To a stranger, he looked as if he was not paying attention, but I knew that expression. He was deep in thought.

"Your statement was so detailed," he said at last,

"that you have left me very few questions to ask. There is one, of the most utmost importance, however. Did you tell anyone that you had this special task to perform?"

"No one."

"Not Miss Harrison here, for example?"

"No. I had not been to Woking between getting the order and carrying it out."

"And none of your family or friends had been to see you?"

"None."

"Did any of them know their way about in the office?"

"Oh, yes. All of them had been shown around it."

"Still, of course, if you said nothing to anyone about the treaty these inquiries are irrelevant."

"I said nothing."

"Do you know anything of the commissionaire?"

"Nothing, except that he is an old soldier."

"What regiment?"

"The Coldstream Guards."

"Thank you," said Holmes. "I

have no doubt I can get details
from Forbes. The authorities
are excellent at gathering facts,
although they do not always use
them to advantage." Then, taking
us all by surprise, he remarked,
"What a lovely thing a rose is."

Holmes walked past the sofa
to the open window and held up
the drooping stalk of a moss rose.
It was a new side of his character
to me, for I had never before seen
him show any interest in natural
objects.

"All other things – our powers,

our desires, our food – are necessities of life. This rose is an extra. Its smell and its color are an enhancement of life, and not an essential. We can find comfort in the natural world."

Percy Phelps and his nurse looked at Holmes with surprise

and a good deal of disappointment on their faces. He stood dreamily with the moss rose between his fingers. It was some minutes before the young lady spoke.

"Do you see any hope of solving this mystery, Mr. Holmes?"

"Oh, the mystery," he said, coming back to the present. "Well, the case is certainly very complicated, but I can promise you that I will look into the matter and let you know any thoughts I have."

"Do you see any clue?"

"You have given me seven, but of course I must test them before I can know of their value."

"Then go to London and test your conclusions," she said.

"Your advice is excellent, Miss Harrison," said Holmes, rising. "I think, Watson, we cannot do better. Do not allow yourself false hopes, Mr. Phelps. The affair is a very tangled one."

"I shall not rest until I see you again," said Phelps.

"Well, I'll come out by the same

train tomorrow, although it's more than likely that I shall have nothing to report."

"God bless you for promising to come," said Percy. "It gives me comfort to know that something is being done. By the way, I have had a letter from Lord Holdhurst."

"Ha! What did he say?"

"He was cold but not harsh. I dare say my severe illness prevented him from being that. He repeated that the matter was very serious, but he added that no steps would be taken about my job until

I was well again."

"Well, that was reasonable and considerate," said Holmes. "Come, Watson, for we have a good day's work before us in town."

Mr. Joseph Harrison drove us to the station, and we were soon heading back to London on the train. Holmes had sunk into deep thought and hardly opened his mouth until we had passed Clapham Junction.

I had just become lost in thought myself when Holmes spoke, startling me. "I suppose that man Phelps does not drink alcohol?"

"I do not think so."

"Nor do I, but we must take every possibility into account. The poor man has certainly got himself into very deep water, and it's a question whether we shall ever be able to get him ashore. What did you think of Miss Harrison?"

"She is a woman of strong character."

"Yes, she is a good sort. She and her brother are the only children of the owner of a forge in

Northumberland. Phelps became engaged to her when traveling last winter. She came down to be introduced to his family. Her brother Joseph accompanied her. Then came this trouble. She stayed to nurse Phelps, and her brother stayed on too. I've been making a few inquiries, you see. But today must be a day of investigations."

I had not planned to spend the day with Holmes. "My practice–" I began.

"Oh, if you find your own cases more interesting than mine–" said Holmes, somewhat harshly.

"I was going to say that my practice could get along very well without me for a day or two, since it is a quiet time of year," I continued.

"Excellent," he said with a smile. "Then we'll look into this matter together. I think that we should begin by seeing Forbes. He can probably tell us all the details we want until we know how to approach this case."

"You said you had a clue?"

"Well, we have several, but we can only test their value by further inquiry. The most difficult crime to solve is the one that has no purpose. Now this one is not purposeless. Who would benefit from it? There is the French ambassador, there is the Russian ambassador, there is any person who might sell it to either of these, and there is Lord Holdhurst."

"Lord Holdhurst!"

"Well, it is just possible that a politician might find himself in a position where he was not sorry to have such a document *accidentally* destroyed."

"Surely not a politician with his honorable record?"

"It is a possibility that we cannot afford to disregard. We shall see the noble lord today and find out if he can tell us anything. Meanwhile, I have already set my inquiries in motion."

"Already?"

"Yes, I sent a telegram from Woking Station to every evening paper in London. This advertisement will appear in all of them."

He handed me a sheet torn from a notebook. On it was scribbled in pencil:

£10 reward. The number of the cab that dropped a fare at or about the door of the Foreign Office in Charles Street at a quarter to ten on the evening of May 23rd. Apply 221B Baker Street.

"You are sure that the thief came in a cab?"

"If not, there's no harm done. But if Mr. Phelps is correct in stating that there are no hiding places either in the room or in the corridors, then the person must have come from outside. If he came from outside on such a wet night, and left no trace of damp on the floor, which was examined within a few minutes of his passing, then it is very probable that he came in a cab."

"It sounds likely."

"That is one of the clues of which I spoke. It may lead us to something. And then, of course, there is the bell – which is the most distinctive feature of the case. Why did the bell ring? Was it the thief who did it out of bravado? Or was it someone who was with the thief in order to prevent the crime? Or was it an accident? Or was it …?" Holmes sank back into the state of

73

silent thought from which he had emerged, but I was accustomed to his moods, and it seemed to me that some new possibility had suddenly dawned on him.

It was twenty past three when we reached our station and, after a hasty lunch at the buffet, we continued on at once to Scotland Yard. Holmes had already sent a telegram to Forbes. We found him waiting to meet us. He was a small man with a sharp and rather unfriendly expression. His manner was very cold toward us, especially when he heard why we had come.

"I've heard of your methods before now, Mr. Holmes," he said, tartly. "You are ready enough to use all the information that the police can give you, and then you try to finish the case yourself and make them look bad."

"On the contrary," said Holmes. "Out of my last fifty-three cases my name has only appeared on four, and the police have had all the praise on forty-nine. I don't blame you for not knowing this.

You are young and inexperienced, but if you wish to succeed in your new duties, you will work with me, not against me."

"I'd be very glad of a hint or two," said the detective, suddenly adopting a much friendlier tone. "I've certainly had no praise from the case so far."

"What steps have you taken?"

"Tangey, the commissionaire, has been followed. He left the Guards with a good character and we can find nothing against him. His wife is a bad lot, though. I fancy she knows more about this than it appears."

"Have you followed her?"

"We have set one of our women to watch her. Mrs. Tangey drinks, and our detective has interviewed her twice but could get nothing out of her."

"I understand that they have had debt collectors in the house?"

"Yes, but they were paid off."

"Where did the money come from?"

"That was all right. The commissionaire got his wages. They have not shown any signs of sudden wealth."

"What did his wife say when you asked why she answered the bell when Mr. Phelps rang?"

"She said that her husband was very tired, and she wished to help him."

"Well, certainly that would

agree with his being found a little later asleep in his chair. There is no proof that they had anything to do with the missing documents? Did you ask her why she hurried away that night?"

"She was later than usual and wanted to get home."

"Did you point out to her that you and Mr. Phelps, who started at least twenty minutes after her, got to her house before her?"

"She explains that by the difference in speed between a bus and a hansom cab."

"Did she make it clear why, on reaching her house, she ran into the kitchen?"

"Because she had the money there with which to pay off the debt collectors."

"She has at least an answer for everything. Did you ask her whether she met anyone or saw anyone loitering about Charles Street when she left?"

"She saw no one but the constable."

"Well, you seem to have cross-examined her pretty thoroughly.

What else have you done?"

"The clerk, Gorot, has been followed all these nine weeks, but without result. We can show nothing against him."

"Anything else?"

"Well, we have nothing else to go on – no evidence of any kind."

"Have you formed a theory about how that bell rang?"

Forbes shook his head. "Well, I must confess that it beats me. Whoever it was, it was bold of them to give the alarm like that."

"Yes, it was an odd thing to do,"

said Holmes. "Many thanks to you for what you have told me. If I can find the culprit, you shall hear from me. Come along, Watson."

"Where are we going now?" I asked as we left the office.

"We are now going to interview Lord Holdhurst, the Cabinet minister and future prime minister of England."

We were fortunate to find Lord Holdhurst still in his rooms in Downing Street. The politician received us with old-fashioned courtesy and seated us on two luxurious chairs on either side of the fireplace. Standing on the rug between us, with his slight, tall figure, his sharp features, thoughtful face, and curling gray hair, he looked like a true nobleman.

"Your name is familiar to me, Mr. Holmes," he said, smiling. "And, of course, I cannot pretend not to know the reason for your visit. There has only been one occurrence in these offices that could call for your attention. Who are you working for, may I ask?"

"For Mr. Percy Phelps," said Holmes.

"Ah, my unfortunate nephew! You can understand that our family relationship makes it even more impossible for me to protect him in any way. I fear that the incident must have a very bad effect upon his career."

"But what if the document is found?"

"Ah, that, of course, would be different," said the lord.

"I have one or two questions that I wish to ask you, Lord Holdhurst."

"I shall be happy to give you any information I can."

"Was it in this room that you instructed Percy Phelps to copy the document?"

"It was."

"Then you could hardly have been overheard?"

I looked around as my friend spoke. It was a vast wood-paneled room. The main desk was in front of the window with two chairs in front of it, and two wooden filing cabinets along a wall on the right. The cabinet in which the treaty had been kept was near the desk.

"It is out of the question," answered Lord Holdhurst.

"Did you ever mention to anyone that you intended to have the treaty copied?"

"Never."

"You are certain?"

"Absolutely."

"Well, since you never told anyone and Mr. Phelps never told anyone, nobody else knew anything of the matter. This means the thief's presence in the room was accidental. He saw his chance and he took it."

Holmes paused. "There is another important point that I wish to discuss with you," he said. "You feared that if the details of this treaty became known, serious problems would follow."

A shadow passed over the politician's face. "Very serious problems indeed."

"And have they happened?"

"Not yet."

"If the treaty had reached the French or Russian embassies, you would expect to hear about it?"

"I should," said Lord Holdhurst.

"Since nearly ten weeks have passed and nothing has been heard, is it fair to suppose that the treaty has not reached them?"

Lord Holdhurst shrugged. "We can hardly believe, Mr. Holmes, that

the thief took the treaty in order to frame it and hang it up."

"Perhaps he is waiting for a better price."

"If he waits a little longer he will get no price at all. The treaty will cease to be secret in a few months."

"That is very important," said Holmes. 'Of course, one could suppose that the thief has had a sudden illness ..."

"A brain fever, for example?" said the politician, flashing a swift glance at him.

"I did not say that," said Holmes, calmly. "And now, Lord Holdhurst, we have already taken up too much of your valuable time. We shall wish you good day."

"And I wish you every success with your investigation," said the minister, showing us out of the room.

"He's a fine fellow," said Holmes as we came out onto Whitehall. "But he struggles to keep up his position. He is far from rich. You noticed, of course, that his boots had been resoled? Now,

Watson, I won't keep you from your patients any longer. I shall do nothing more today, unless I have an answer to my cab advertisement. But I would be extremely obliged if you would come down with me to Woking tomorrow, by the same train that we took today."

I agreed, and we went off in different directions.

The next morning, I met him as planned and we went to Woking together. Holmes told me that there had been no answer to his advertisement. No fresh light had been thrown upon the case. From his expressionless face, I could not tell if he was disappointed with the lack of progress of the case. His conversation, I remember, was about an entirely different topic.

We found our client still under the charge of his devoted nurse but looking much better than before. Percy rose from the sofa and greeted us without difficulty.

"Any news?" he asked, eagerly.

"My report, as expected, is a negative one," said Holmes. "I have seen Forbes and I have seen your uncle. I have also set one or two trains of inquiry in motion that may lead to something."

"You have not lost heart, then?"

"By no means."

"God bless you for saying that!" cried Miss Harrison. "If we keep our courage and our patience, the truth must come out."

"We have more to tell you than you have for us," said Phelps, reseating himself on the sofa.

"I hoped you might have something."

"Yes, we have had an adventure during the night." His expression grew very grave as he spoke. A look of something like fear sprang up in his eyes. "I am beginning to believe that I am the center of some monstrous conspiracy! My life is threatened as well as my honor!"

"Ah!" cried Holmes.

"It sounds incredible, for I have not, as far as I know, an enemy in the world. Yet from last night's experience, I can come to no other conclusion."

"Please let me hear it."

"Last night was the first night that I have slept without a nurse in the room. I felt so much better that I thought I could dispense with her. Well, about two in the morning I had sunk into a light sleep when I was suddenly aroused by a slight noise. It was like the sound that a mouse makes when it's gnawing a plank. I lay listening to it for some time, thinking that it really was a mouse. Then it grew louder and suddenly, from the window, I heard a sharp metallic *snick*. I sat up in amazement. There could be no doubt what the sounds were now. The first ones had been caused by someone forcing an instrument in the slit between the sashes, and the second by the catch being pressed back."

I was amazed at this story, but Holmes sat nodding slightly, as if he had expected this to happen.

Percy continued. "There was a pause, as if the person was waiting to see whether the noise had awoken me. Then I heard a gentle creaking as the window was very slowly opened. My nerves are not what they used to be. I sprang out of bed and flung open the shutters. A man was crouching at the window! I could see little of him, though, for he was gone like a flash. He was wrapped in some sort of cloak that came across the lower part of his face. One thing I am sure of is that he had some weapon in his hand. It looked to me like a long knife. I distinctly saw the gleam of it as he turned to run."

"This is most interesting," said Holmes. "What did you do then?"

"I would have followed him through the open window if I had been stronger. As it was, I rang the bell and woke up the house. It took some time because the bell rings in the kitchen and the servants sleep upstairs. I shouted, though, and that brought Joseph down. He woke up the others. Joseph found marks in the flower bed outside the window, but the weather has been so dry lately that it was impossible to follow the trail across the grass. There's a place on the wooden fence that skirts the road that shows some clue, they tell me. It looks as if someone has climbed over and snapped the top of the rail in doing so. I have said nothing to the local police yet. I thought that I had better have your opinion first."

This tale appeared to have an extraordinary effect upon Holmes. He rose from his chair and paced about the room in uncontrollable excitement.

"Misfortunes always come in groups," said Phelps, smiling bravely. It was evident that his adventure had somewhat shaken him.

"You have certainly had your share," said Holmes. "Do you think you could walk round the house with me?"

"Oh, yes, I should like a little sunshine. We'll ask Joseph to come too."

"And I also," said Miss Harrison.

"I'm afraid not," said Holmes, shaking his head. "I think I must ask you to remain sitting exactly where you are."

The young lady sat back down, but she did not look pleased. Her brother joined us, then all four of us set off together. We walked round to the outside of Phelps' window. There were marks in the flower bed, just as he had said, but they were hopelessly blurred and vague.

Holmes stooped over them for an instant, and then rose, shrugging his shoulders.

"I don't think anyone could make much of this," he said. "Let's go round the house and see why this particular room was chosen by the burglar. I should have

thought those larger windows of the drawing room and dining room would be more attractive."

"They are more visible from the road," suggested Joseph.

"Ah, yes, of course. There is a door here that he might have attempted. What is it for?"

"It's for tradespeople and deliveries. It's locked at night."

"Have you ever had an alarm like this before?"

"Never," said our client.

"Do you keep anything in the house that would attract burglars?"

"No."

Holmes strolled around the house carelessly with his hands in his pockets. This was a world away from the precise, energetic man I was used to. I frowned at the odd behavior.

"By the way," he said to Joseph, "you found some place, I understand, where the fellow scaled the fence. Let us have a look at that."

The young man led us to a spot where the top of one of the wooden rails had been cracked.

A small fragment of wood was hanging down. Holmes pulled it off and examined it critically.

"Do you think this was done last night? It looks rather old, does it not?"

Phelps looked at it closely. "Well, possibly so."

"There are no marks of anyone jumping down on the other side. No, I don't think we'll find anything more here. Let us go back to the bedroom and talk the matter over."

Percy Phelps was walking very slowly, leaning on the arm of his future brother-in-law. Holmes walked swiftly across the lawn, and we were at the open window of the bedroom long before the others.

"Miss Harrison," said Holmes, speaking urgently to the lady inside the room. "You must stay where you are all day.

Let nothing distract you. Do not tell anyone that I have asked you to do this. It is of vital importance."

"Certainly, if you wish it, Mr. Holmes," said the girl in astonishment.

"When you go to bed, lock the door of this room on the outside and

keep the key. Promise to do this."

"But Percy?"

"He will come to London with us."

"And I am to remain here?"

"It is for his sake. You can help him. Quick! Promise!"

She gave a quick nod just as the other two gentlemen arrived.

"Why do you sit there moping, Annie?" cried her brother. "Come out into the sunshine!"

"No, thank you, Joseph. I have a slight headache. This room is deliciously cool and soothing."

"What do you propose now, Mr.

Holmes?" asked our client.

"Well, in investigating this minor affair, we must not lose sight of our main inquiry. It would be a great help to me if you would come up to London with us."

"At once?"

"Well, as soon as you can. Say, in an hour."

"I feel strong enough, if I can really be of any help."

"The greatest possible."

"Perhaps you would like me to stay there tonight?"

"I was just going to propose it."

"Then if my attacker returns, he will find my bed empty. We are all in your hands, Mr. Holmes, and you must tell us exactly what you would like us to do. Perhaps you would prefer that Joseph come with us to look after me?"

"Oh, no. My friend Watson is a medical man, you know, and he'll look after you. We'll have our lunch here, if we may? Then we shall set off for town together."

It was arranged as Holmes suggested. Miss Harrison excused herself from leaving the bedroom, in accordance with Holmes' instructions. What my friend's plan was I could not tell, unless it was to keep her away from Phelps, who was happy to be getting stronger and hopeful that the case would soon be solved. He joined us for lunch in the dining room. Holmes had a still more startling surprise for us. After accompanying us down to the station and into our carriage, he calmly announced that he had no intention of leaving Woking.

"There are one or two small

points that I would like to clear up before I go," he said. "Your absence, Mr. Phelps, will in some ways assist me. Watson, when you reach London, you would do me a great favor by driving at once to Baker Street with our friend here, and remaining with him until I see you again. Mr. Phelps can have the spare bedroom tonight, and I will be with you in time for breakfast. There is a train that will take me into Waterloo at eight."

"But how about our

investigation in London?" asked Phelps, looking disappointed.

"We can do that tomorrow. I think that at present, I will be of more use here."

"You might tell them at Briarbrae that I hope to be back tomorrow night," cried Phelps, as we began to move from the platform.

"Oh, I don't expect to go back to Briarbrae," answered Holmes, and waved to us cheerily as we moved out from the station.

114

Phelps and I talked it over on our journey, but neither of us could find a good reason for this change of plan.

"I suppose he wants to find some clue about the burglary last night, if a burglar it was. I don't believe it was an ordinary thief."

"What is your own idea, then?"

"You may put it down to my weak nerves, Watson, but I believe that there is some deep political intrigue going on around me. For some reason I don't understand, my life is in danger from conspirators. It sounds absurd, but consider the facts. Why would a thief try to break in at a bedroom window, where there could be no hope of any theft? And why would he come with a long knife in his hand?"

"You are sure it was not a crowbar?"

"Oh, no, it was a knife. I saw the flash of the blade quite distinctly."

"But why on earth should you be targeted?"

"Ah, that is the question!" cried Phelps.

"Well, if Holmes takes the same view, that would account for his action, would it not? Presuming that your theory is correct, if he can lay his hands upon the man who threatened you last night, he will have gone a long way toward finding the naval treaty. It is absurd to suppose that you have two enemies, one of whom robs you, while the other threatens your life."

"But Holmes said that he was not going to Briarbrae."

"I have known him for some time," I said, "but I never knew

him to do anything without a very good reason."

In the cab back to Baker Street, we turned to other topics of conversation. It was a weary day for me. Phelps was still weak after his long illness. His misfortune made him irritable and nervous.

In vain, I tried to
interest him in stories
of my time in the army or
anything that might take
his mind off his problems.
He would always come back to
the lost treaty, wondering what
Holmes was doing, what steps
Lord Holdhurst was taking, or
what news we would have in the
morning. As the evening wore
on, his nervousness became quite
painful.

"You have absolute faith in
Holmes?" he asked.

"I have seen him do some remarkable things."

"But surely he has never exposed such a dark plot as this?"

"Oh, yes. I have known him solve questions with fewer clues than yours."

"But not where such large interests are at stake?"

"To my certain knowledge, he has acted on behalf of three of the reigning houses of Europe."

"But you know him well, Watson. He is such a mysterious fellow that I never quite know what to make of him. Do you think he is hopeful? Do you think he expects to make a success of it?"

"He has said nothing."

"That is a bad sign."

"On the contrary. I have noticed that when he is off the trail, he generally says so. It is when he is on a scent, but not absolutely sure yet that it is the right one, that he is most distant and quiet."

I rose from my chair. "Now, my dear fellow, we can't help matters by making ourselves nervous about them. Let me advise you to go to bed and be fresh for whatever may await us tomorrow."

Phelps agreed, although I knew from his excited manner that there was not much hope of sleep for him. His mood was infectious. I lay tossing and turning half the night myself, brooding over this strange problem. I invented a hundred theories, each more impossible than the last. Why had Holmes remained in Woking? Why had he asked Miss Harrison

to stay in the sickroom all day? Why had he been so careful not to let the people at Briarbrae know that he intended to stay near them? I wracked my brains until I fell asleep still trying to find some explanation that would cover all these facts.

It was seven o'clock when I awoke, and I immediately went to Phelps' room to find him tired after a sleepless night. His first question was whether Holmes had arrived yet.

"He'll be here when he promised,"

I said, "and not an instant sooner or later."

My words were true. Shortly after eight, a hansom cab dashed up to the door and our friend got out. We saw that his left hand was wrapped in a bandage and that his face was very grim and pale. He entered the house, but it was some time before he came upstairs.

"He looks like a beaten man," said Phelps.

I was forced to confess that he was right. "After all," I said, "the clue of the matter probably lies here in town."

Phelps gave a groan. "I had hoped for so much from his return. But surely his hand was not tied up like that yesterday. What can be the matter?"

"You are not wounded, Holmes?" I asked as my friend entered the room.

"Tut, it is only a scratch through

my own clumsiness," he answered, nodding his good mornings to us. "This case of yours, Mr. Phelps, is certainly one of the darkest that I have ever investigated."

"Won't you tell us what has happened?" I asked.

"After breakfast, my dear Watson. Remember that I have had a fair journey this morning. I suppose that there has been no answer to my cabman advertisement? Well, well, we cannot expect to score every time."

The table was all laid. Just as I

was about to ring, Mrs. Hudson
entered with the tea and coffee.
A few minutes later, she brought
in three covered dishes, and we
all drew up to the table. Holmes
was ravenous, I was curious, and
Phelps was in the gloomiest
state of depression.

"Mrs. Hudson has risen to the occasion," said Holmes, uncovering a dish of curried chicken. "What have you here, Watson?"

"Ham and eggs," I answered.

"Good! What are you going to take, Mr. Phelps – curried fowl or eggs?"

"Thank you. I could not eat a thing," said Phelps.

"Oh, come! Try the dish before you."

"I would rather not."

"Well, then," said Holmes, with a mischievous twinkle in his eye. "I suppose that you have no objection to helping me?"

Phelps reached out to the nearest dish and lifted the cover. As he did so, he uttered a scream, and sat there staring. His face was as white as the plate upon which he looked. Across the center of it lay a little roll of blue-gray paper. He caught it up and then danced wildly about the room, pressing it to his chest and shrieking out in his delight. Then he fell back into an armchair, limp and exhausted by his own emotions.

"There, there!" said Holmes soothingly, patting him on the shoulder. "It was too bad to spring it on you like this, but Watson here will tell you that I never can resist a touch of the dramatic."

Phelps seized his hand and kissed it. "God bless you!" he cried. "You have saved my honor."

"Well, my own was at stake too,

you know," said Holmes. "I assure you it is just as hateful to me to fail in a case as it can be to you to blunder over a task."

Phelps put away the precious document into the innermost pocket of his coat.

"I have not the heart to interrupt your breakfast any further," he said, "yet I am dying to know how you got it and where it was."

Holmes swallowed a cup of coffee and turned his attention to the ham and eggs. Once he had finished his meal, he rose, lit his pipe, and settled himself down into his chair.

"I'll tell you what happened," he said. "After leaving you at the station, I went for a walk through some lovely Surrey countryside. I stopped at a pretty little village called Ripley and stayed there until evening. I went back to Woking, and arrived in the road outside Briarbrae just after sunset.

"Well, I waited until the road was clear, and then I climbed over the fence and into the grounds."

"Surely the gate was open!"

exclaimed Phelps.

"Yes, but I chose the place where the three fir trees stand. I got over without any chance of being seen by anyone in the house. I crouched down among the bushes on the other side and crawled – look at the terrible state of my pants knees – until I had reached the clump of rhododendrons just opposite your  bedroom window. There I kneeled down and waited.

"The blind was not drawn in your room, and I could see Miss Harrison sitting there reading

  133

by the table. It was quarter past ten when she closed her book, fastened the shutters, and went to bed. I heard her shut the door and felt quite sure that she had turned the key in the lock."

"The key!" said Phelps.

"Yes. I gave Miss Harrison instructions to lock the door on the outside and take the key with her when she went to bed. She carried out every one of my instructions perfectly. Certainly without her help, you would not have that paper in your coat pocket.

"The night was fine, but it was still very tiring and very long. Almost as long, Watson, as when you and I waited in that deadly room when we looked into the problem of the Speckled Band."

I remembered, of course, and a shudder went down my spine. It had been one of the most frightening nights of my life. We had waited for the killer to strike without knowing how they would do so.

Holmes gave a small smile and

continued. "There was a church clock in Woking that struck every quarter of an hour, and I thought more than once that it had stopped. At last, at about two in the morning, I suddenly heard the gentle sound of a bolt being pushed back and the creaking of a hinge."

Holmes paused, enjoying the drama of his tale. Phelps and I waited, hardly daring to breathe.

"A moment later the servants' door was opened, and Mr. Joseph Harrison stepped out into the moonlight."

"Joseph!" cried
Phelps.

"He had
a black coat
thrown over his
shoulders so that
he could hide
his face if he was
seen. He walked
on tiptoe under
the shadow of
the wall, and
when he reached
the window, he
put his knife

through a crack in the shutters, thrust the bar up, and swung them open.

"From where I lay I had a perfect view of the inside of the room and all his movements. He lit

the two candles that stood on the mantelpiece, and then he began to turn back the carpet near the door. Then he kneeled and pulled out a square piece of the floorboard. It was a loose piece to enable access for plumbers or the like. Out of this hiding place, he drew that little roll of paper, pushed the board back, straightened the carpet, blew out the candles, and walked straight into my arms as I stood waiting for him outside the window.

"Well, he's more vicious than I

thought, that Master Joseph. He flew at me with his knife, and I got cut over the knuckles before I had the upper hand. He looked at me murderously out of the one eye he could see out of when I had finished. But he listened to reason and gave up the papers. Having got them, I let him go, but I sent a telegram to Forbes this morning with all the details. If he is quick enough to catch his bird, then that is all well and good. But if, as I suspect, he finds the nest empty, all the better for the government.

I think that both Lord Holdhurst and Mr. Percy Phelps would much prefer that the affair never got as far as the police courts."

"My God!" gasped our client. "Are you telling me that during these ten weeks of agony, the stolen papers were in the very room I was sleeping in all the time?"

"Yes."

"And Joseph! Joseph a villain and a thief!"

"I'm afraid Joseph's character is rather more dangerous than one might think from his appearance.

From what I've heard from him this morning, I gather that he has lost a great deal of money on the stock market and that he is willing to do anything to recover the money. He is a very selfish man, so when a chance presented itself, he didn't worry either about his sister's happiness or your reputation."

Percy Phelps sank back in his chair. "My head whirls," he said. "Your words have dazed me."

"The main difficulty in this case," said Holmes, "lay in

the fact that there was too much evidence. What was vital was hidden by what was unimportant. I had already begun to suspect Joseph from the fact that you had intended to travel home with him that night. It was likely that he should call for you. He also knew the Foreign Office well. When I heard that someone had been anxious to get into the bedroom, where no one but Joseph could have hidden anything, I became certain – especially as this happened on the first night that the nurse was not there. This showed that the intruder knew the ways of the house."

"How blind I have been!"

Phelps looked so ashamed that I put my hand upon his arm. "It's clear to see now that it has been explained," I said.

"Of all the facts presented to us, we had to choose those that

were essential," said Holmes. "That was the difficulty, and this is what happened: Joseph Harrison entered the office through the Charles Street door. Since he knew his way, he walked straight into your room and entered the instant after you left it. Finding no one there, he rang the bell. At that instant he caught sight of the document on the table. A glance

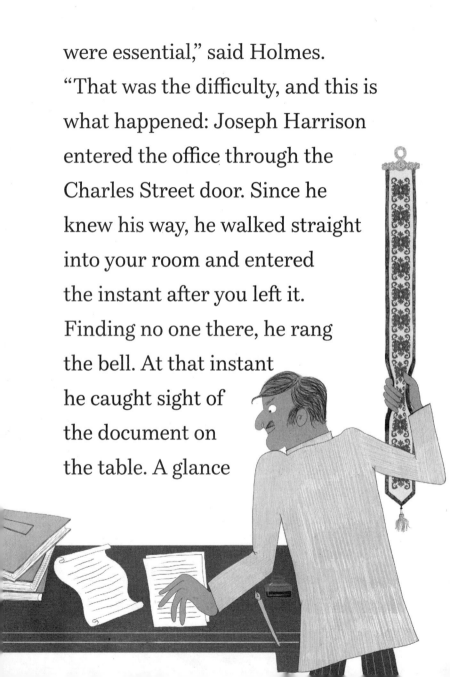

showed him that this was a state document of great value. In an instant, he had thrust it into his pocket and was gone. A few moments passed, as you remember, before the commissionaire drew your attention to the bell. That was just long enough to give the thief time to escape.

"He made his way to Woking by train. Then he hid it in what he thought was a very safe place. After a day or two, he planned to take it to the French Embassy, or whoever would pay the best price.

Then came your sudden return. Without a moment's warning, he was bundled out of his bedroom. From then onward there were always at least two of you there to prevent him from regaining his treasure. It must have been a frustrating situation, but at last he had his chance. The night he tried to creep in through the window, you were awake because you had not taken your usual sleeping pills."

"I remember."

"I suspect he made sure there

was a large enough dose to keep
you asleep. He must have been
surprised that you were not. Of
course, I knew that he would
try again whenever he had the
opportunity. Your leaving the
room yesterday gave him his
chance. I asked Miss Harrison
to stay in it all day so that he
would not suspect. Then, having
given him the idea that the coast
was clear, I kept guard as I have
described. I already knew that the
papers were probably in the room,
but I had no wish to rip up all the

floorboards searching for them. I let Mr. Harrison take them from their hiding place and so saved myself a lot of trouble."

"Why did he try the window when he could have come in through the door?" I asked.

"To reach the door he would have to pass seven bedrooms. On the other hand, he could get out onto the lawn with ease. Anything else?"

"Do you think that he wanted to harm me?" asked Phelps. "Or only to use the knife as a tool?"

Holmes shrugged. "I can only say for certain that Mr. Joseph Harrison is a gentleman who I would be extremely unwilling to trust."

The case resolved, we all three sat down to a hearty breakfast.

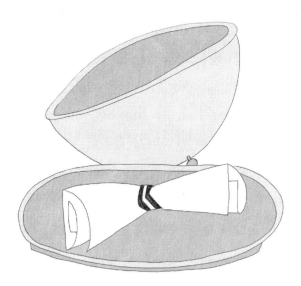

Sherlock Holmes

World-renowned private detective Sherlock Holmes has solved hundreds of mysteries, and is the author of such fascinating monographs as *Early English Charters* and *The Influence of a Trade Upon the Form of a Hand.* He keeps bees in his free time.

Dr. John Watson

Wounded in action at Marwan, Dr. John Watson left the army and moved into 221B Baker Street. There he was surprised to learn that his new friend, Sherlock Holmes, faced daily peril solving crimes, and began documenting his investigations.

Dr. Watson also runs a doctor's practice.

To download Sherlock Holmes activities, please visit
www.sweetcherrypublishing.com/resources